peninsula
**connections**
for early childhood

## PCEC "1000 X 5"
### Children's Book
### Recycling Project

Reading with children each day can contribute to their early success in school. By the time your child enters Kindergarten, you and he or she may have read <u>more than</u> 1000 books together! Please accept this book as a gift and a reminder of the value of establishing routine book-sharing experiences. We hope this book may become one of many books in your home library or that you will consider recycling it and others you wish to donate through your neighbourhood school.

The PCEC "1000 X 5" Project is sponsored by Beacon Community Services/Peninsula Connections for Early Childhood in partnership with Saanich School District, Success by 6®, United Way of Greater Victoria, and the Victoria Foundation. Our work is also supported by the Peninsula Co-op Food Centre, Beacon Books, ORCA Book Publishers, the Rotary Literacy Round Table and Discover Books; as well as individuals, service clubs, and many family-serving agencies on the Saanich Peninsula.

# POCKET ROCKS

*To see a world in a grain of sand*
*And a heaven in a wild flower.*
*—William Blake*

For Ian and children of all ages who need the safety of secret worlds
and for "J.B." and all BJs who work so hard and understand.
*—S.F.*

For my niece, Cerys.
*—H.F.*

**National Library of Canada Cataloguing in Publication Data**

Fitch, Sheree

Pocket rocks / Sheree Fitch; Helen Flook, illustrator.
ISBN 1-55143-289-7
I. Flook, Helen  II. Title.

PS8561.I86P62 2004          jC811'.54          C2004-902449-3

First published in the United States 2004
**Library of Congress Control Number**: 2004105789

**Summary:** Found rocks help Ian Goobie cope with troubles at school.

Orca Book Publishers gratefully acknowledges the support for its publishing programs provided by the following agencies: the Government of Canada through the Book Publishing Industry Development Program (BPIDP), the Canada Council for the Arts, and the British Columbia Arts Council.

Design by Lynn O'Rourke
Scanning: Island Graphics, Victoria
Printed and bound in China

Orca Book Publishers
Box 5626 Stn. B
Victoria, BC  Canada
V8R 6S4

Orca Book Publishers
PO Box 468
Custer, WA   USA
98240-0468

07 06 05 04 • 4 3 2 1

ORCA BOOK PUBLISHERS

# POCKET ROCKS

Story by Sheree Fitch

Illustrations by Helen Flook

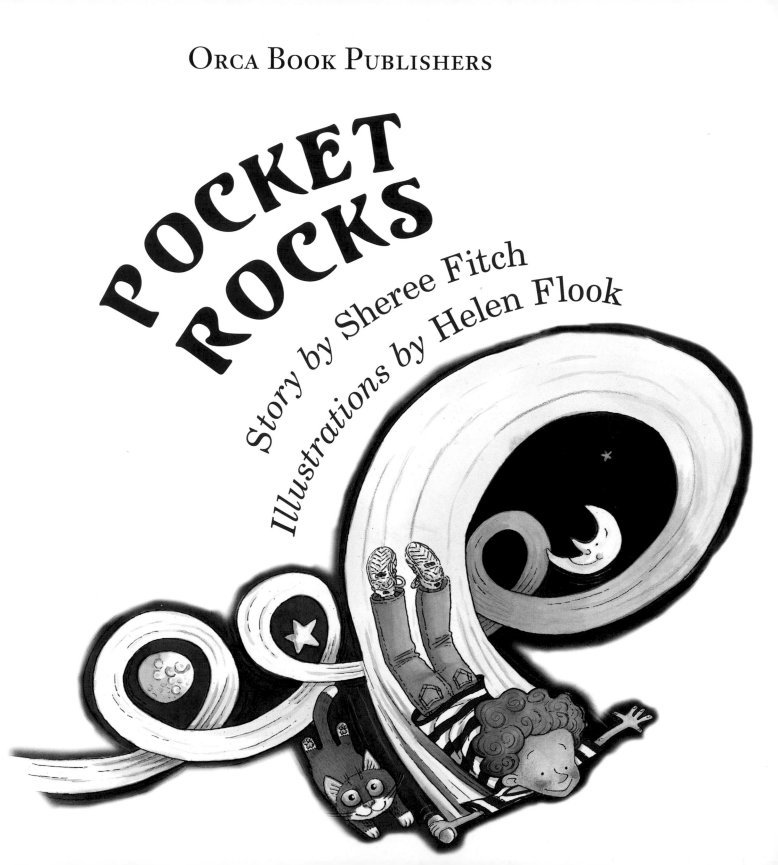

There once was a boy named Ian Goobie.

Every morning, he looked into the mirror to say hello to himself.

His chin was pointy and his forehead was wide.

"Just like an upside-down triangle," he said. And scrunched up his nose. *Scrunch, scrunch, scrunch.*

Every morning, Ian Goobie knocked on his head. *Knock, knock.* "Time to come out!" he said.

He brushed his hair. "Soft as dandelion fuzz or a whisper."

Ian Goobie smiled his widest smile.

"Ian, time for school," called his mother.

Ian Goobie's smile drooped and wobbled and turned into a scribbly line.

The thing of it was, Ian wished every day was someplace else. Or summertime. Or Saturday. He wished he could go anyplace else but school.

It wasn't his teacher. He liked Mrs. Dingle. Mrs. Dingle's voice was marshmallow and she smelled like lemon shampoo.

He liked BJ too. His eyes were as brown and kind as melting chocolate chips. But even with BJ's help, no matter how hard Ian Goobie tried, he could not do the things everyone else could do.

"Ian!" called his mother in her *hurry up*! voice.

Ian Goobie wanted to crawl inside the mirror and stay there all day. Instead, his hands turned into a sad little butterfly. He waved good-bye to himself.

And went to school.

Day after day was the same until the morning Ian found a rock. A rock the size and shape of an egg but not white. A rock as black as shoe polish still in the tin and speckled all over with teeny white freckles.

Ian picked up the rock. It was smooth and cool against his cheek.

Ian sniffed the rock. Sometimes smells made pictures in his head.

Ian closed his eyes. *Swish, swoosh, swish*! Ian was flying
in a tunnel of wind. He looped and spiraled and dipped and
swooped until he landed in an emerald green jungle. Ian
opened his eyes. "Jungle Rock," he said with a giggle.

Ian cradled the rock in his hand. "Rock-a-bye, rock-a-bye,
rock-a-bye rock," he whispered. When he was sure the rock
was fast asleep, he tucked it into his pocket. His left pocket.
And went in to school.

That day, Ian tried his hardest ever when it was time for printing. BJ helped. But every line that was meant to stand up, fell down. Every line that was meant to be straight, curled like the curliest hair on Ian Goobie's head. Ian Goobie got a fluttery feeling in his belly, as if a small bird were in there, trying to get free.

Then he remembered. Inside his pocket was a whole other world. Thinking of Jungle Rock made the fluttery feeling go away. Ian Goobie smiled. And kept trying to print.

Every day for many days, Ian put rocks in his pockets.
Moon Rock and King Rock, Turtle Rock and Tiger
Rock, Kangaroo Rock and many, many more.

*Swish, swoosh, swish!* With every rock he flew away in a tunnel of wind and landed in whole other worlds. When he opened his eyes, he whispered to each and every rock, "Rock-a-bye, rock-a-bye, rock-a-bye rock."

When he was sure they were all fast asleep, he tucked them into his pockets.

Left and right.

ROAR

In school, his pencil was still not much of a friend. He tried to make a tent with legs and it turned into a vase. He put flowers in it. He tried to make a mountain and a valley, but it turned into a Z.

But when his heart pounded or his head filled with too much noise, he remembered his rock-a-bye rocks.

They were his friends. *Swish, swoosh, swish!* They flew him away in tunnels of wind

Day after day was the same.

Until the day of the disaster.

until he landed in whole other worlds

At recess, Ian was making something for BJ with his rock-a-bye rocks. The bell rang, but Ian Goobie wasn't finished. That was bad enough.

But things got worse. Fast as he could, Ian Goobie scooped up the rocks he hadn't used, stuffed them into his pockets and ran toward the rest of the class.

Too many rocks. Ian Goobie had stuffed too many rocks in his pockets, and while he was running, his

pants

fell

down.

Ian stopped. Stone still. Somebody laughed.

"Ian Goobie's got rocks in his head. His pants fell down and his face is red!" shouted Trevor. He was the fastest printer and reader in the whole class.

"SHHH!" Mrs. Dingle said. "That's enough!" Her voice was hard as burnt marshmallow.

Ian Goobie never remembered much about the next fifteen minutes. Except his voice was a siren. BJ took him to the quiet room. He waited until Ian stopped being a fire engine. He waited until there was nothing left to blow from Ian Goobie's nose.

"Now let's go back to class," BJ said. "We've got a visitor."

Ian took BJ's hand, but he kept his head down just in case he could find a rock-a-bye rock. Of course, there were none to be found.

The visitor looked like an upside down capital T. His hair was the color of squash. Ian did not like squash. His beard looked like a small broom stuck to his chin.

"Some stories are read, some stories are said and some stories rhyme," said the man in a trumpety voice. "Once upon a time," he began.

He told story after story after story.

Ian closed his ears. He closed his eyes. "I want my rock-a-bye rocks!" he hissed.

"Later, Ian," said BJ. "I promise. When the stories are over."

But when the stories were over, the children had questions.

"How long have you been collecting stories?" asked Sue Ellen.

"For a long time," said the man. "But when I was a boy, I collected rocks. Always had rocks in my pockets. Still do." He reached into his pocket and held one up.

Ian stared at the man with the rock in his hand. He nodded his head up and down. BJ looked at the man. The man looked at BJ. They nodded their heads too.

It was Ian's turn, with BJ's help, to tell *his* story. The man scratched his whiskers when Ian got to the part about his pants falling down. He whispered a secret in Ian's ear.

"Your whiskers tickle," said Ian. "They're not scratchy like a broom at all." The storyteller laughed and laughed. And gave Ian the rock.

Everyone clapped. Even Trevor.

As always, BJ kept his promise.

He took Ian outside to pick up his rock-a-bye rocks. "Let's put them in a can for now, Ian," he said.

But Ian tugged at BJ's arms.

"Over there," he said.

Ian worked so hard that he bit his tongue. Then he stood back so that BJ could see his present.

The straight line of rocks hardly squiggled. The tent was a tent with legs, not a vase filled with flowers. And instead of a Z, he had made a mountain and a valley.

"I-A-N!" shouted BJ. "IAN! You did it!" BJ picked Ian up and swirled him around and around in a tunnel of wind.

Nowadays, Ian Goobie keeps rocks all over his house. He keeps them in boxes and cans and baskets. He has a pouch for rocks that Mrs. Dingle made especially for him. He still keeps a few rocks in his pockets.

And he never worries about his pants.

*This story is a true story although I changed it some, and Ian Goobie is a real boy although I did not use his real name. And I am the storyteller who found out Ian's story of the rocks and the falling-down pants, but I do not have squashy hair or wear polka-dot suspenders.*

*I do have piles of rocks in corners all over my house, for I have learned that rocks, like stories, have secret worlds hidden inside them that make me feel safe.*

—Sheree Fitch